The Other Carly

AMY LAURENS

OTHER WORKS

SANCTUARY SERIES

Where Shadows Rise
Through Roads Between
When Worlds Collide

KADITEOS SERIES

How Not To Acquire A Castle

STORM FOXES SERIES

A Fox of Storms and Starlight

SHORTER WORKS

Bones Of The Sea
Darkness And Good
Dreaming Of Forests
It All Changes Now
Of Sea Foam And Blood
Rush Job
Trust Issues

NON-FICTION

How To Write Dogs
How To Theme
How To Create Cultures
How To Create Life
How To Map
The 32 Worst Mistakes People Make About Dogs

Find other works by the author at
www.amylaurens.com

The Other Carly

INKLET #70

AMY LAURENS

Inkprint PRESS

www.inkprintpress.com

Print ISBN: 978-1-925825-77-0
eBook ISBN: 9798201649371

www.inkprintpress.com

National Library of Australia Cataloguing-in-Publication Data
Laurens, Amy 1985 –
The Other Carly
50p.
ISBN: 978-1-925825-77-0
Inkprint Press, Canberra, Australia
1. Young Adult Fiction—Fantasy—Contemporary 2. Young Adult Fiction—Fantasy—Dark Fantasy 3. Young Adult Fiction—Horror 4. Young Adult Fiction—Short Stories, Collections & Anthologies

First Print Edition: November 2021
Cover photo © Jills via Pixabay
Cover design © Inkprint Press
Interior art © Amy Laurens

THE OTHER CARLY

THE DOOR TO MY HIDING PLACE SLID open and I burrowed deeper under my arms against the old plywood tabletop that had been the only furniture in the run-down wilderness tree-fort for the last five years.

"Joanna Richards," said a voice that was whisperingly familiar. "My how the mighty do fall."

Footsteps, then a warm pressure against my side. I cracked an eyelid open to peek at the boy from under my arm, to see if the face would remind me why I knew the voice.

Decently-muscled shoulders, long-ish neck, dark hair... My eyebrows lowered. I couldn't see his face, but that jawline definitely reminded me of someone.

He shifted. "You've grown up."

Ah. Not a boy. Ryan.

I sighed and pressed my face back against the faint wood smell of the tabletop. "If you've come to patronise me," I said, "don't. My day has been shite enough as it is."

He was quiet for a second, then drew a little away. "Sorry. I didn't mean it like that. It's just, the last time I saw you, you were thirteen and be-rating the house mistress who tried to punish you for shinning out the dorm window." He snickered, then gave a contented little sigh. "Her face is et-ched into my memory for all time."

In spite of myself, I smiled a little. "Yeah. That was a good moment."

"Yeah." He drifted away for a moment into a happy little reverie. "But anyway, moving on. What's up with you? Why are you in here? I thought we only used this place when the parents came to visit." He sat bolt upright. "They're not in town, are they? Because my folks are with me, and if—"

I pushed myself out of my slump and rolled my neck. "Dude, chill. No parents. It's fine."

His brow wrinkled. "Then why are we in here?"

I shrugged one shoulder and stared at a stain on the counter. "I went to Carly Davies' party today."

Ryan raised an eyebrow. "We like her now?"

"Pft." I cut him a look. "What do you take me for?"

"So why did you—Oh." Glum understanding clouded his face. "It goes like this: you pick someone easy—"

"Hey!"

"Alright, someone you were friends with then, a long, long time ago, but who saw you once for what you really are and did the smart thing and ditched you.

"Only you can't believe that's true, even now, and so you invite them, and beg and plead, and promise you'll be friends again, that you've seen the error of your ways and if only they would *just come* to your *party*," Ryan said in his best falsetto, clasping his hands under his chin and fluttering his eyelashes, "the rainforests will stop disappearing and climate change will be averted.

"Only then, when they come, you laugh. You laugh loud and long, and all your cronies laugh too, and you tell yourself that they deserve it because they ditched you—but really it's because you're empty inside."

He straightened. "Am I right?"

My lips twisted as I swallowed a chuckle. I'd forgotten how easily he could wring laughter from me. I made a note to let him do it again sometime. "Close," I said. "Or you could just invite the whole year on Facebook and then, when your stupid ex-friend's curiosity gets the better of her and she shows up—*then* you laugh." I gave Ryan a wry smile. "Pretty dumb, huh."

Ryan nudged my shoulder with his. "No. Not dumb."

I dangled my feet off the edge of the chair and stared at the tiles. For a second—no, less than that, half a second—for half a second when I'd arrived at Carly's giant, white-picketed, tall-oaked, gable-roofed mansion of perfection, it had felt like old times, like I was six again and nothing else in the world mattered except that I was about to walk into the most amazing house I'd ever seen in my life. For just that half second, I could imagine what a friendship between a grown-up Carly and a grown-up Joanna might look like.

And then Maddy had spotted me, looked me up and down as she towered below me on stilettos longer than my arms that allowed her to just surpass five foot, and she'd said the fatal words, and the whole party had turned to give me that look, one part shocked, two parts cruel mockery, and four parts like the most disgusting insect in the world had stood up and spoken.

Although given Carly was scared of moths and thought they were putrid, and given I kind of liked them, all cute and fuzzy with feathery antennae as they were, that bit could have been worse. I sighed.

"Come on," said Ryan, grabbing my hand and hauling me to my feet. "Let's go eat some ice cream."

I stared glumly at my bowl, chinking my spoon absently against my water glass. Not even peach and coconut gelato had been able to lift my mood.

Ryan shifted, and as I glanced up he caught my eye. "There is this one thing," he said slowly, as though the words were heavy and fragile and had to be put down with great care.

"What one thing?" I was pretty sure nothing he could suggest would make me happier today, but it was sweet of him to try.

When he met my eyes again, his were aflame. "I've learned things since I've been gone. I can control it now. You could have it—revenge."

I shrugged, feigning nonchalance because the burn that started with that word seemed too terrible to own.

Revenge.

Eight long years of petty hatreds stacked themselves up and up until Carly's head toppled from them all. Goosebumps rose on my arms; I told myself it was only the unfortunate combination of ice cream and aggressive air conditioning.

"Well?"

Ryan's cheeks were flushed, and I realised I hadn't responded. "Yeah," I said, toying with my spoon. "Maybe."

His chair scraped back against the tiled floor and he stood, hands white against the tabletop. "I need more than a maybe," he whispered tightly. "You know where to find me."

He left, a used spoon, half a blood orange sundae and six dollars sixty-five the only indication he'd been present.

I called him of course.

His cell number hadn't changed since he'd got it in eighth grade and although it had been over a year since I'd dialled it last, I still knew the number. Deleting him as a phone contact had made surprisingly little difference when it came to deleting him from my life.

I guess I'd always known one day that it would come to this. I'd never told him that he was most of the reason Carly and I weren't friends anymore, because she loathed him in the special and precise way of the weak fearing the powerful, and because I had always defended him. Right up until Jenna Thomson's head had splattered on the pavement, anyway.

I'd known what he was, of course. And I'd never denied it to Carly, either.

I just didn't agree that it made him a monster.

Now, as I stared at my reflection in the bathroom mirror, eyes a little too wide and fingers a little too white as they clutched the phone, I had to wonder if that was only because I was a monster too.

He picked up on the fifth ring. "Yeah?"

Was I imagining it, or did my eyes turn a little green? "I'll do it," I said. I held my breath, waiting for an answer, and when I ran out of air I gulped it in greedily, like maybe oxygen was rationed for people who did evil.

"Okay," he said, and when he spoke, it was like icy water crashing down over my head, like nerves or excitement or dread. "Meet me on the corner of Raeburn and Fifth. You know the place."

I did. I just hadn't expected to go there ever again. "Now?" I said, ignoring the way my voice went squeaky around the edges, and hoping that he would too.

"Why not?" I heard the inward rush of air as he opened his mouth to say something else, but nothing came.

"What?" I said, the rough scratch on the phone's casing where I'd dropped it a week ago jagging my skin. "What is it?"

Another deep breath. "Now," with finality. "The less time you have to think about it, the better. Trust me."

I didn't ask why. I didn't need to.

"We're not going to splatter her on the concrete though, right?" I asked from my vantage point in the lowest fork of the old oak, voice barely shaking at all.

Ryan paused mid-circle to cut me a filthy look. "That's right, bring that back up again why don't you. Anything else you'd like to say, while we're on the topic?"

I shifted on my perch. "Well I was just checking!"

He sniffed, shaking his head and resuming the circle he was drawing on the path, blue chalk streaking his fingers. He completed it and stepped back, scuffed some out and redrew it to make it more circular, then surveyed it again. "I *have* been learning," he said, not looking up.

I stared at him. "Ryan, it's okay. I trust you."

He glanced up, surprised written in his eyes. Maybe he really didn't know that I'd defended him.

I shrugged. "What now?"

He pointed to a small wooden bowl he'd placed in the circle. "Ideally we'd get a hair or an eyelash or something, and put it in the bowl to anchor the spell. But we can also just write her name. That usually works okay."

I pulled out the tiny notebook I kept in my jacket pocket for emergencies, along with a miniature pen. "This do?"

Ryan nodded, and I scrawled out "Carly" in a pretty cursive font I'd learned from my grandmother.

Funnily enough, I don't think she would have disapproved of it being used to curse someone. I got the feeling that she'd have been cursing people left, right and centre, if only she'd known how. I slipped from the tree and folded the paper in half before handing it to Ryan.

He stretched over the circle and dropped it into the bowl, then wiped his fingers on his shirt as though the paper had stained him.

"What now?" I asked.

"Go back to the tree." His jaw was tight and strained, and I thought about asking whether he was okay, whether he was up for this, but instead I shrugged and climbed back up to my perch.

Ryan began to shuffle around the circle, mumbling under his breath. For two full circuits, nothing happened except that his voice grew louder. He started the third circuit. Magic rose like mist from the circumference of the circle, wispy blue and red, rising up to about three feet before spiralling in to meet over the centre. Ryan shouted the final word, and gold streaked up from the bowl to meet the fog, the paper fluttering, shivering, then bursting into ash.

The lights spiralled upwards, half a foot thick, three quarters, a full foot, taller and taller until it stretched half the height of the giant, old oak.

My fingers knotted around a fistful of oak leaves.

The magic swirled and swivelled, catching its bearings.

Then it swooped—

Straight at me.

My eyes widened and panic clawed at my chest as I remembered the one little secret I'd never told him, the thing that had never seemed important because I'd only been a baby, too young for it ever to have mattered: my name was Carly, too.

But my parents, my adoptive parents who'd had me since I was three months old, had called me by my middle name—Joanna—because Carly, the other Carly, the bigger, brighter, better Carly, had been there first.

Magic engulfed me and I thrashed. *I'm not the one you want! It's not me!*

But the magic didn't listen. It bound me tighter and tighter; no matter how hard I struggled, I stayed stuck fast.

Panic welled up, the hot burn of adrenalin in my stomach, my throat.

Help.

I couldn't even squeeze my eyes

shut. Couldn't swallow down the fear choking my throat, my thoughts.

Then Ryan was there, eyes like ghosts as he squeezed my unresponsive shoulders. "I'll fix it," he said grimly. "I'll fix it. I swear."

THE MAKING OF
THE OTHER CARLY

I wrote this piece as a kind of echo-response to another short story I read around the time, if I recall correctly. My story was for the old Darkness & Good blog, back when Liana Brooks and I were doing a weekly-ish story challenge.

The original story either had the idea of magic going for the wrong person, or else of two people with the same name who were mistaken tragically for each other—I can't remember which way around it is. But either way, the idea of names in magic, of name magic, has always fascinated me, and this story presented a way to play with that idea, and of the very real consequences that might occur if you had name-based magic and weren't *quite* precise enough with your instructions.

I imagine something like this is the entire reason last names were invented. Ha.

I think, were I to write in this story world today, it would be just as dark, if not more so. After all, if you have a world where magic remembers the name your parents gave you, what happens to people who legally change their name? Does the magic learn the new name, too, or are you perpetually haunted by this spectre of the past?

On the one hand, if magic only knew you by your birth name, changing your name would provide some form of protection.

On the other, it would make it that much harder for those who wish to leave their birth name behind to ever truly divorce themselves of that part of their identity.

And that might be a very dark story indeed.

Read more by Amy Laurens!

A FOX OF STORMS AND STARLIGHT

CHAPTER ONE

SIX YEARS AGO, I SAVED a fox in the bush. It was only because my dog died. At the time, it felt like a pretty crappy bargain.

It was the first day of autumn—not by the calendar, but by the fresh bite in the morning air, the golden quality of the light as it lit the main road through town in the mid-afternoon.

Sailor was a big, black shaggy thing, something like a Newfoundland, a lively shadow in the golden light, and I was eleven.

I'm sorry to be starting any story this way, but the fact of the matter is, this where it all began.

I'll spare you the awful details. Enough to say that Sailor had got out of the yard somehow, and had been hit by a smallish truck careening down the highway that split our tiny town in two as it blatantly ignored the speed limit.

I saw it happen.

And although I cradled him in my lap as the smell of burnt-out brakes and hot asphalt and turning leaves filled my nose, his giant, furry black head all of him I could hold, there was nothing I could do.

There was nothing anyone could do.

I knew that, but it didn't stop the knot of frustration and guilt in my chest, or the taste of bile in the back of my throat every time I closed my eyes and saw the truck hitting him, again and again and again.

It took years for that vision to fade.

But that evening, only a few hours after it had happened, everything still felt fresh, and raw.

Sunny, my sister, was only nine at the time. She cried for hours, just sobbing like she'd never breathe right again.

I'd cried a little, at the scene with Sailor's head lying in my lap as his big, brown eye stared up at nothing.

It had been mercifully fast, there was that.

And the driver had copped a massive fine—speeding, reckless driving, I think they even defected his truck—and came to visit us later, a big, pot-bellied man standing on our front verandah, shuffling his royal blue cap round and round and round in his hands as he apologised.

But that evening, with Sunny sobbing her heart out on the couch in the living room and Mum and Dad trying desperately to console her as dinner burned on the stove, I couldn't cry, even though the acrid scent of burning soy sauce, scorching brown sugar and smoking rice wine from the marinade prickled the back of my throat and the corners of my eyes.

I was the eldest, and I had to be responsible.

Possibly, if I'd been just a little more responsible, Sailor wouldn't have died.

So I slipped out the glass slider from the family room to the deck while Sunny cried, glancing up at the two storeys of our moody grey house behind me before jumping down the three steps from the rail-less deck to the lawn, and set out for the gate in the back fence.

I couldn't cry, and I didn't want to add anything to an already chaotic and stressful situation inside—but I couldn't stay there, either.

In the gaps between the gum trees to the west, the sky tinged to red and gold at the horizon, the sun sinking slowly into oblivion. I'm pretty sure I didn't know the word oblivion back then, but I knew what it meant, how it felt—and I craved it, desperately.

Anything would be better than the gaping hole in my chest.

And so, because I didn't know where to find it or how to get there, I stalked through the bush, pushing myself until I breathed hard and my lungs ached and sweat ringed me, chasing the way that hard exercise elevated me over my constantly looping thoughts.

Directly above, dark, heavy clouds obscured the sky, and the air was thick, heavy, humid.

Beneath the smell of dry gum leaves and even drier dirt, I could catch a hint of ozone, and occasionally the wind turned cool for a breath as it gusted against my skin, promising a late evening storm.

I strode harder, faster, outpacing the video looping in my mind of the truck's impact.

When the first drops of rain spat at me from out of the sky, I barely noticed. My skin was filmed with sweat, slick and salty, and the peppering of rainwater barely added to it.

That was at first.

But within minutes, it became clear that those first pattering spits had been the early foreshadowing of a storm darker and more intense than any I remembered.

Thunder rolled across the sky, distant and grumbling at first, a lazy background chorus to the rhythmic melody of the rain as it splattered down on grey-green leaves and red-tinged twigs, turning the silvered bark of an old, dead gum to deep grey and making the spiky, tussocky grass seem oddly luminescent in the dying light.

I stood under a grey gum with stains down its trunk that the rain was turning orange, arms wrapped around myself, shivering hard—and for the briefest instant, thought about not going home.

Mum and Dad would pitch a fit.

And I had to be responsible.

I turned, dark t-shirt plastered to my skin, dark hair sticking to my face and clinging to my neck, and began trudging my way back.

The storm closed over properly, clouds rolling over the horizon and cutting off the thin scythe of blood-coloured sunset, making the bush dark and unwelcoming in the premature night.

Lightning flashed.

Thunder cracked hot on its heels.

I jumped—and stared hard at the gap between two ghost-barked trees, where for a second, I was sure I'd seen a pair of eyes.

Nothing moved.

Nothing except the drenching rain, anyway, weighing down the branches that tossed fitfully in the wind.

My pulse slowly calmed.

The rumours we'd all grown up with, indoctrinated since both, spoke of something strange and dark... but in the forest north of here, in the pines, the plantation—not here, not in the natural, native bush.

I shivered.

The smell of wet dirt and soaked bark rose around me, undercut by eucalypt and ozone.

If anything had the power to wash away the hurt inside me, this storm was it. I tipped my face to the sky, imagining that the rain washing over me had the ability to wash me inside as well, and the raindrops splattered hard on my cheekbones, my chin, my tightly closed eyelids.

More lightning. More thunder, cracking over the constant hiss of the falling rain.

And in the distance, something eerie, lifting the hairs on the back of my neck: a strange kind of high-pitched howl, a cry that rang with moonlight and distance, cutting straight through the noise of the storm.

Bolts of lightning streaked across the sky—one—two—three—in the space of half a second, followed immediately by a growling crack of thunder so immense it vibrated in my chest.

I ducked down instinctively into a crouch.

There, in the corner of my eye...

I froze, crouched with my arms over my head.

The strange cries came again—and they were closer.

I stared hard at the place, low to the ground, where I was sure I'd seen something small, maybe the size of a cat.

Flash. Growl.

Rain spitting down.

There. Right there. A small animal, pointy ears, light coloured chin and throat...

The strange, eerie cries came a third time, and my heart pounded fiercely. Whatever was making the noise, it was close. Really close.

The little creature across from me reacted too, flattening itself to the ground.

My jaw twitched.

My heart pounded.

My fingertips bit into my upper arms.

Stay? Go?

Run? Freeze?

The hairs on my neck prickled again and goosebumps broke out all over me.

Cold dread formed a knot in my stomach.

Something was coming.

Something worse than the storm.

I had to get home.

I made it halfway to standing—and a series of strange, awful noises made me freeze again. They were sharp, clacking, squealing sounds, like someone knocking two echoing stones against each other, interspersed with high-pitched yowling...

The creature in the darkness screamed.

I threw my back against the gumtree behind me, pressing hard against it.

My heart hammered.

I peered back and forth in the dark, eyes wide.

Rain drenched down, but my throat was dry.

My pulse pounded faster.

The little creature screamed again—and as lightning flashed, I saw it on its back, legs slashing wildly as something attacked.

The awful, clicking-yowling noises sounded right in front of me.

I slapped my hands over my ears, gasping. Water ran down my face, getting into my mouth, my eyes.

It was hurting.

Whatever the small thing was, it was getting hurt, and I'd seen enough animals hurting today.

Something in my chest snapped.

I flung myself across the ground, leaping a couple of tussocks and a fallen branch before I crashed to my knees.

I crawled closer, desperate, gasping for air through the heavy curtains of rain.

I couldn't see it. Where?

Somewhere here, near the base of that tree...

The yowling screeched right next to my ear. I cowered against the ground, spiky grass pricking my face, wet-earth smell smothering me—but now, there was a strange mustiness too, a cousin to wet-dog smell.

At the next flash of lightning, I saw it.

The creature was a fox—and something barely visible was attacking it, only the gleam of eye or flicker of teeth visible in the gloom.

But the damage was real enough.

The little fox's side had been opened right up, and in the bright, stark flashes of heavenly electricity, the blood was dark, thinned by the constant rain.

No. No more animals were going to die today.

Not when this time, I could do something about it.

I snatched at a branch on the ground that turned out to be more of a glorified twig, and launched myself toward the creature.

I had no idea what was attacking it, but I screamed and waved my handful of twiggy leaves anyway, batting them in the air over the fox like I knew what I was doing.

The horrible clacking cries ceased abruptly.

With one long, low rumble, the rain began to ebb.

I poised, waiting.

But nothing came.

The attackers were gone.

Still gasping for air, pulse galloping in my throat, I sat next to the fox and shifted it carefully into my lap, realising as I tasted salt that I was crying.

I huddled over, trying to shelter the poor creature from the slackening rain, running my fingers over its wiry cheek—over and over and over and over.

"Please," I sobbed, throat tight and aching, chest constricted. "Please. Please don't die. Please."

Please, I prayed to anything that might be listening. *No more death. Not today.*

Not today.

Another gust of cool air washed over the clearing, taking the last of the rain with it—and lifting the goose-bumps on my arms again.

And as it did, I could have sworn I heard a voice. *Neither do I wish him to die now.*

I shivered, drawing the fox close, like it was a stuffed animal I could hug for comfort—its comfort or mine, I couldn't say. I glanced around the dripping bush, eyes wide. The rumours spoke of an evil presence, and I could easily believe that might be what had attacked the fox.

But a voice? No one had ever mentioned a voice.

There was nothing to be seen, and anyway the voice had sounded kindly—and didn't want the fox to die.

Assuming I hadn't just imagined it, of course. Which, half-drowned by grief, the other half drowned by the storm... An over-active imagination seemed highly likely.

Can you fix him? I thought it hard, though, just in case someone really was listening.

Something shifted in my lap.

Around us, the world stilled, dazed from the storm, but also something more, something watching, something waiting, as the bush held its collective breath.

The only sound was the occasional drip of rainwater from the gum leaves onto a fallen log—no insects, no wind, no rustling of leaves.

Just… stillness.

And the fox, who shivered in my lap.

The clouds tore open, revealing a ragged triangle of stars that glittered in the fox's eye as it blinked open and stared up at me.

My chest snagged.

My throat ached from crying, and a headache was forming in the back of my head.

But the fox blinked up at me—alive.

I ran a finger down it again, from nose to cheek to ear to shoulder, all the way down its side to its thick, bushy tail—and the wound in its side began to close.

Laboriously, it hauled itself to its front legs.

I tried to stop it—"No, it's okay, you can stay here, I'll look after you"—but it lifted its top lip to show half-hearted teeth, and staggered away.

As it did, I thought perhaps its fur began to shrink.

And suddenly, it looked larger in the night—as large as a dog, as large as Sailor…

But I blinked, and it was just a trick of the light, because the creature that darted away into the bushes like nothing was wrong at all was clearly a fox, the size of a large cat or maybe a small beagle, and nothing more.

And if something screamed in the night not long afterward, and the cry sounded horribly, horribly human?

Well.

I was halfway back toward home again by then, and I pressed my fingertips to my lower eyelids and prayed my parents wouldn't murder me for getting home so late.

ABOUT THE AUTHOR

AMY LAURENS is an award-winning Australian author of fantasy fiction for all ages. She has never actually put a curse on anyone's name yet, although maybe writing someone into a story as a villain sort of counts, so you should probably beware, if you know her.

Amy has written the award-winning portal-fantasy *Sanctuary* series about Edge, a 13-year-old girl forced to move to a small country town because of witness protection (the first book is *Where Shadows Rise*), the humorous fantasy *Kaditeos* series, following newly graduated Evil Overlord Mercury as she attempts to acquire a castle, the young adult series *Storm Foxes*, about love and magic and family in small town Australia, and a whole host of non-fiction.

INKLETS

Collect them all! Released on the 1st and 15th
of each month.

INKLET #055
Allure
AMY LAURENS

INKLET #056
The LIES We KNOW
LIANA BROOKS

DOUBLE
INKLET #057
AFTERMATH & Fool Me Once
AMY LAURENS

INKLET #058
Purity
An Age Of Unicorns Story
AMY LAURENS

INKLET #059
Saved
AMY LAURENS

INKLET #060
A Kiss is the Secret
AMY LAURENS

INKLET #061
A Changing Tides Story
Fire Bright
AMY LAURENS

INKLET #062
Hades AND Persephone
LIANA BROOKS

INKLET #063
Just So Long As You're Happy
AMY LAURENS

INKLET
#064
Theft Of A Lifetime
LIANA BROOKS

INKLET
#065
Shoe
AMY LAURENS

INKLET
#066
Published AUTHOR
LIANA BROOKS

DOUBLE ISSUE
INKLET
#067
THE REMARKABLE INSIGHT OF JELLYBEANS & Understanding
AMY LAURENS

INKLET
#068
Desperate Measures
AMY LAURENS

INKLET
#069
Rock-a-bye
LIANA BROOKS

INKLET
#070
the Other Carly
AMY LAURENS

INKLET
#071
Bs By Bioluminescent light
AMY LAURENS

INKLET
#072
Even Villains Grant Wishes
A Heroes & Villains Story
LIANA BROOKS